The Pocket Dogs

Written by Margaret Wild

Illustrated by Stephen Michael King

SOUTHWOOD
B O O K S

Mr Pockets had a very big coat, and in his very big coat he had two very big pockets.

The two very big pockets were just the right size for two very small dogs. Their names were Biff and Buff.

Every day, winter or summer,
Mr Pockets put on his big coat.
Then he put Biff in the right pocket,
and Buff in the left pocket.

"Are you ready?" he always asked.
"Are you happy?"

Biff and Buff always said, "Ruff! Ruff!",
which meant, "Yes, thank you,
Mr Pockets!"

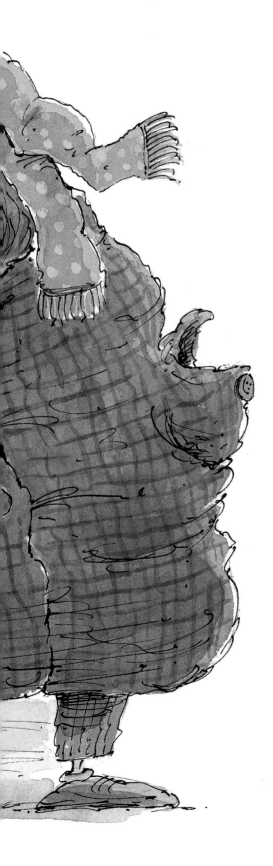

So off they went to do the shopping.

Mr Pockets and Biff and Buff always took the
long, interesting way to the shops.
As they walked along, people said:
"Hello, Mr Pockets!"
"What big pockets you have, Mr Pockets!"

"Hello, little pocket dogs!"
"Hello, Biff! Hello, Buff!"

Biff and Buff always said hello most politely.

Then one day Biff stuck his foot
through a small hole in
Mr Pockets' right pocket.

In no time at all
the hole grew
bigger

and bigger

and bigger!

Biff couldn't tell Mr Pockets about the hole
in the pocket. But he could tell Buff.

Buff said, "One day you will fall out of the
pocket. On to the ground. On to your head.
And you will be lost."

"Ruuuuuuuff!" said Biff.

That night Biff had a bad dream.

He dreamed that he fell out of the pocket.

He dreamed that he looked and looked for
Mr Pockets and Buff, but he couldn't find
them anywhere.

He woke up, feeling cold and alone.

The next morning Biff hid under the bed,
but Mr Pockets found him.

Biff hid among the socks and the undies,
but Mr Pockets found him.

Biff hid in Mr Pockets' hat,
but Mr Pockets found him.

"What's the matter with you today,
Biff?" said Mr Pockets.

Biff tried to tell him. Buff tried to tell him. But Mr Pockets didn't know what they were saying.

Mr Pockets put Biff in his right pocket, and Buff in his left pocket.

"Are you ready?" he asked.
"Are you happy?"

Buff said, "Ruff! Ruff!" But Biff
couldn't say anything. His mouth
was full of coat.

Off they went to do the shopping.

"Are you all right there, Biff?" said Buff.

Biff opened his mouth to say, "No, not really" –
and out of Mr Pockets' pocket he fell. On to
the ground. On to his head.

When Biff looked up, he saw legs. Lots and lots of legs. But he couldn't see Mr Pockets' legs.

"Ruuuuuuff!" said Biff.

A lady with a shopping basket stopped. She said, "Hello, little dog. Are you lost? I will try to find your home."

The lady put Biff in her basket, and off they went.

But Biff didn't like being
a shopping basket dog.

He was a pocket dog.
Mr Pockets' pocket dog.

So Biff jumped out of
the basket, and ran away.

A small girl who was pushing a toy pram said,
"Look, Mum. There's a little lost dog."

"We'll put him in your pram," said her mum.
"We'll try to find his home."

So Mum and the small girl put Biff in the pram,
and off they went.

But Biff didn't like being
a toy pram dog.

He was a pocket dog.
Mr Pockets' pocket dog.

So Biff jumped out of
the pram, and ran away.

"Hello, hello," said a man with a shopping trolley. "I nearly trod on you! Come with me and I'll try to find your home."

The man put Biff in his shopping trolley, and off they went.

But Biff didn't like being
a shopping trolley dog.

He was a pocket dog.
Mr Pockets' pocket dog.

So Biff jumped out of the
trolley, and ran away.

"Ruuuuuuuuuuff!" said Biff.

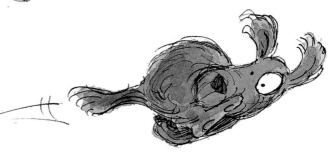

He shut his eyes, tucked his tail between his legs, and put his head on his paws.

"Ruuuuuuuuuuuuuff!" said Biff.

Then Biff felt someone pick him up,
and hold him tight.

"There you are!" said Mr Pockets. "Buff and I have
been looking everywhere for you!"

Mr Pockets tucked Biff into his coat,
and took him home.

Biff and Buff watched Mr Pockets
get out a needle and cotton and
sew up the very big hole in the
right pocket.

"Did you fall on to the ground?" asked Buff.
"Yes," said Biff.
"On to your head?" asked Buff.
"Yes," said Biff.

"You were lost, weren't you?" said Buff,
and he licked Biff's ear to show he was sorry.

"Yes, I was lost," said Biff. "For a while I was a
shopping basket dog, then a toy pram dog, then
a shopping trolley dog. But now I am found.
I am a pocket dog. Mr Pockets' pocket dog."

And he jumped on to Mr Pockets' lap and
wriggled into his shirt, against his heart.